Claw:
An Alien Scifi Romance

DEMELZA CARLTON

ONE

Baking was so much easier than practicing law, Claw told himself as he pummelled the bread dough. No matter how frustrating legal clients got, you could never, no matter how obnoxious they were, never ever punch them. Bread, though, seemed to expect it.

So when the cream order had failed to

arrive for the second week in a row, due to the loss of the Colony's sole dairy herd, and no one had any idea how long it would be before their replacements matured enough to give milk… He'd had to learn to make his own butter using powdered milk and a variety of other ingredients before he could even start on tomorrow's croissants. The croissants, in turn, had taken twice as long as usual because the butter substitute hadn't been chilled enough the first three times he'd tried, and even on the fourth try, he'd had to only make small batches because if the accursed stuff got too warm, the croissants wouldn't hold their shape, so he had to stop everything to whisk the trays into the cool room the moment they were full…

Or the strawberry order hadn't arrived because it had been involved in an aircar crash between Eden and Metropolis, and the rescue workers had prioritised rescuing people over precious food supplies. Claw knew that food could be replaced, albeit with synthesised substitutes, seeing as strawberries were still in short supply, but having to rehydrate three crates of accidentally freeze dried strawberries that were supposed to be fresh so he could make them into strawberry tarts…

In the end, he'd had to give up on the tarts entirely, and spend hours rehydrating the (deliberately) freeze dried apple pieces so that he could turn both kinds of fruit into pies. People expected their strawberries to be slightly soggy once they'd been baked inside a pie, while they were less forgiving about them turning to jam on top of their tarts.

Maybe he should have actually turned them into jam, and used them in cream buns or doughnuts or something. If only the Colony hadn't run out of cream…

Claw punched the bread again. By the time he was done, these would be the most well-kneaded loaves in the Colony.

Then again, supply shortages being what they were with the Colony only having been established for a year and agriculture limited to what they could grow quickly in the unfamiliar soils of New Hope, the Bear Claw Bakery was the ONLY bakery in the Colony, and therefore his was the only bread to be bought in it.

But food made from Colony-grown ingredients, especially fresh food, sold at a premium when ration bars were free to all colonists, and when people paid a high price for their bread or croissants or whatever other pastries he managed to make, they expected it to be good, or they wouldn't buy it again.

Claw sighed. Sourcing supplies, supply chain disruptions, pricing, marketing, planning which products to make…so many things he didn't know about running a bakery. He'd never had to worry about any of this when he was working part time as a baker's assistant back on Tito. He'd just done everything the bakers ordered him to, and it had worked.

Maybe he needed an assistant or an

apprentice here, to do the actual baking while he worried about the business side of things.

But that would be like giving up, and going back to practicing law. If he'd wanted to keep doing paperwork, he'd have stayed working for the Senate, drafting new laws with which they could govern all the people of the Altan System.

Besides, he didn't actually make enough profit yet in the bakery to justify hiring anyone new. Sure, if there were two bakers they could make and sell twice as much product, in theory, but only if they had enough ingredients.

Ooh, which reminded him – if he didn't have enough cream to do the bear claws, he'd have to mix up a batch of mock cream next. Much like the butter substitute, it worked best if it had chilled for a few hours in the cool room before he piped it into the pastries. Claw ducked into the cool room to check.

Yes, he'd need to make mock cream after the bread dough was done.

A baker's work was never done.

It was still better than being a lawyer, though. Thrashing out the Altan System Treaty between Titans and Humans in an effort to end the war had been a thousand times more stressful than baking. And that had been without the daily death threats from the Humans First crazies, or the Titan terrorists who called themselves the Anti Robot League.

Not that the Humans had robots, or

AIs of any kind that he'd seen but the ARL had been adamant that Humans were hiding them, somehow, and they would…use them in a surprise attack, or some such insanity.

Now the only crazies he had to deal with were ones who complained there weren't enough almond slivers on their bear claws. He dealt with them by slipping them a few extra, without mentioning that all the almond slivers came from a food synthesiser, because it would be years before any almond orchards in the Colony bore fruit. Or nuts.

But he was supposed to keep the food synthesiser secret, as there weren't many of them in the Colony. His had been salvaged from a ship destroyed during the war, and he'd had to write a lengthy application to the Colony Administration to get the device allocated to him. Even now, he lived in fear of it being reallocated somewhere else, where it was needed more, when half his ingredients still had to be synthesised so he could fill the bakery shelves every morning.

This was what he wanted. His reward for his part in putting the treaty together. A nice, relaxing job with none of the pressures of being an important lawyer. Where he could work at his own pace all night, like the night owl he was, without sitting in endless meetings or having to answer to anyone at all. He ordered his ingredients, they arrived, and he turned them into baked goods that his fellow colonists enjoyed. He could...

His comm beeped, signalling an incoming call.

Claw checked the caller ID. There were some people he still had to answer to, no matter who or what he was.

"Hello?"

TWO

"Hi, Orson. How do you feel about speed dating?"

Claw wasn't sure which set his teeth on edge more – the use of his given name, or the thought of using a matchmaking service like speed dating.

"Allie, you know I prefer to be called Claw now."

She blinked, then shook her head. "Of course, of course. Sorry, Claw, it's just that I called you that for so long while we were negotiating the treaty, it's stuck in my head and just sort of popped out. I'll blame the lack of sleep with a new baby, even if Galen is the stay at home parent and not me. But…speed dating. Have you ever done it?"

No, and he never intended to do that or any other form of professional matchmaking. "Of course not. If I were that desperate for female company, I wouldn't use a dating service. They use stock photos of attractive people to entice lonely singles to join the service, where the reality is that most of them are desperate and dateless for a reason. And as the men usually outnumber the women, I'd have far worse odds finding a potential mate than, say, someone like you would."

Not that she needed to. Everyone in the Colony knew she'd given birth to one of the first Human-Titan hybrid babies, and the child's Human father had moved to the Mer community to take care of it, in accordance with Mer custom.

"It's just that…a few of the Mer girls here are considering settling down with Human partners of their own. They saw an ad for a speed dating service at the One Shot Cantina, the Intergalactic Dating Agency or something, and so they contacted them. Only to be told the service is at full capacity for women looking to breed, but if they knew any men who'd be interested…"

Her pause was so pregnant, it could have given birth to griffon quintuplets.

Talon might be interested.

"Not me," Claw said.

"Yeah, I know that, which is why I called you. Pretend you're still a suspicious lawyer. If a dating service is turning away women, what are your first thoughts?"

Come to think of it, there were alarm bells ringing in his head. Not as loud as when he'd been a practicing lawyer, but… "That's not right. It must be a scam of some sort. Trying to lure desperate men into paying for the service…" No, that couldn't be right. Desperate women's money was just as good as men's. "Is it a front for an illegal brothel?"

"You know the Treaty as well as I do. Brothels aren't illegal as long as everyone's over the age of consent and there is consent. But if the girls are coerced, it's not true consent…"

"Sexual slavery or indentured labour is definitely illegal under the Treaty, just like it was in the Titan system. Surely no one would…" Humans. It had to be Humans. Only they would do such base things no Titan would even dream about.

"That's why I need you to go in there. Tell them you're looking for a potential mate, and ask questions. Ask the girls in the speed dating session. And afterwards, tell me what you find out. Tell me if I'm being paranoid, if the Intergalactic Dating Agency is real and above board and genuinely interested in matching their clients with appropriate partners, or if there's something darker going on. I'll owe you one."

Allie owing him a favour. Now that was valuable. But he couldn't just walk in there and start asking questions. People would automatically think he was one of the Watch, and stop talking to him. Maybe even toss him out.

"Would you mind if I took a couple of friends along? Maybe Talon or Fang or Achilles?" he asked.

"The more eyes, the better," Allie said, echoing his own thoughts. "Take whoever you like. As long as they're as principled as you – because if something dodgy is going on here, the Watch will not take kindly to any man who takes advantage of a girl whose consent is coerced."

"They wouldn't. They're good guys," Claw said.

"I guess we'll see, won't we? Anyway, it's on Friday night. Go, talk to some girls, and get a feel for what's going on, please. That's all I ask."

"And tell you if there's anything suspicious going on, too, of course," he said.

"Of course."

"And you, the Mer Enforcer, will owe me a favour?" Claw tested.

"Mer Enforcer and Colony plumber, don't forget. If your place gets flooded, having a plumber owe you a favour is worth its weight in fusion fuel."

Like when he'd first arrived, and his

apartment floor had been turned into an ice rink due to the combination of a leak and a faulty thermostat. He couldn't thank Allie enough for fixing that mess. "It's a deal."

"Happy speed dating, Orson." She ended the call before he could correct her.

How bad could it be?

THREE

Donna clapped her hands. "Your attention, please, girls."

After a year on Star Farm under Donna's command, she had their attention before she'd even opened her mouth. Well, all except for Iva.

"Iva!"

The youngest girl looked up, all

innocence, like she hadn't head Donna the first time. "Yes, madame?"

Donna's cheeks pinked. "Don't make me put you in solitary," she warned.

Iva merely shrugged. She'd spent more time in the cells than anyone else, but she never seemed to mind. "You do what you must, madame."

Donna looked like she wanted to respond, then shook her head and forced out a smile. Ignoring Iva, she said, "I have wonderful news. We have been invited to a social event at the One Shot Cantina. It's a speed dating event, where you will meet some of the male alien colonists who are looking for brides to bear their children. I don't need to remind you that as part of your contract, you are required to bear four children for the Colony…"

Finally. Franny leaped to her feet. "I volunteer!"

Donna frowned. "I'm not finished explaining yet."

Franny nodded. "I know. We're all listening. But I volunteer. I'd really like to go."

Donna nodded, and continued.

Franny stopped listening. She'd done all the training, spent a year working on this farm, and while farm to table was a really admirable thing, she was more into the final steps before things got to the table, rather than the ones at the beginning of the process. She'd give her right arm for a piece of toast in the morning for breakfast, instead of protein bars. Her right arm and her right foot for a croissant. She'd even bake the things herself, if she had to. Before she handed over her arm, obviously. Kneading bread dough was pretty hard without both arms.

She hadn't left the farm once since she'd arrived. The last time she'd been to a pub was back on Earth, when she and Rue had sneaked out to the spaceport bar to celebrate her eighteenth birthday. She hadn't seen a man since Exodus, let alone gotten naked with one.

Now Donna was sending them to a pub to meet hot aliens? She didn't need to know the details. Of course she was going to volunteer. She wondered if he'd have wings or tentacles or horns or a tail or scales or…

Someone tapped her shoulder,

interrupting her daydreaming.

"You shouldn't volunteer like that," Iva said, plopping into the empty seat beside Franny.

Everyone else had left, so they were the only ones left in the dining hall.

"Why not? I'm twenty-one. I want to go to a pub and hook up with a guy like a normal person instead of working all day and never going out at night," Franny said. "And these are hot alien guys."

Iva just shook her head. "If Donna has found them, then they will probably not be hot."

"It's a pub, and it's a speed dating event. Donna didn't pick them, they signed up with this Intergalactic Dating Agency. Some of them will be awful, sure, but I'm sure others won't be. I mean, haven't you ever hooked up with someone at the pub? Just for a night?"

The moment the words left her lips, she knew they were a mistake. They'd celebrated Iva's eighteenth birthday last week. She hadn't been allowed a trip to the pub, or any alcohol at all.

Iva shook her head. "I already have someone perfect for me. Only my family back on Earth did not agree. He's here, in the Colony."

Iva, the youngest of them all, had already found her perfect match? Wow. Just wow. "Have you seen him? Met up in secret? Oooh, what if he's at this dating thing, so he can see you?"

Iva bowed her head. "I have not seen him since Earth. But perhaps he will be at this pub, yes."

Franny grinned. "I hope so. You'll have to let me do your makeup for you, to make sure you look absolutely amazing. I mean, if it's been over a year since you last saw this guy, you want to absolutely knock his socks off when he sees you, don't you?"

Iva's smile was wistful. "If he sees me. He might not be there."

"Well, if he's not there, then he's an idiot. You might find some hot alien who sweeps you off your feet and makes you forget all about him. Oh, but make sure you take time with the foreplay before you…you know. If it's your first time."

Yep, she shouldn't have said that. Iva's smile turned into a grimace, before she got up and headed for the common room.

Franny sighed and followed her. What else did she have to do at night?

She couldn't wait until Friday.

FOUR

Claw had intended to tell his friends why they were going to the One Shot Cantina, but in the end, it hadn't been necessary. They'd agreed to go as his wingmen, after he'd beaten them all at Go. Something that didn't happen often – both Fang and Talon must have been distracted by work things, and Achilles hadn't even been there. Pity. If he'd been able to persuade Achilles to come, every eye would have been on the natural showman, and no one would notice him asking too many questions.

As it was, he was going to have to pretend to be like one of those old-time trial lawyers who defended criminals in court, back on Earth. A practice which had been abolished when all trials were placed before the Central Intelligence to judge on Tito.

Talon and Fang peeled off, each headed for the girls they were supposed to speed date, whatever that was. But Claw had no idea where he was supposed to go.

"Find your seat, sir, so we can start," the officious faun with the tablet said.

"Those two ladies are not yet taken – perhaps over there?"

Claw followed the faun's pointing fingers. The two ladies were in deep conversation, ignoring everyone else in the room, their heads lowered so he couldn't even see their faces.

What he could see were the numbers on the tables – 1 and 2.

He wavered.

Number Two looked up. "Oh, you definitely need to meet my friend Franny here," she said as she pointed to Number One. "I have particular tastes, and I don't believe you share them." She gave him a knowing wink, which left him even more mystified.

What the…?

Someone shoved him out of the way

to take the seat across from Number Two.

Which left Number One – Franny the friend.

Claw hurried to take his seat. "Hi."

She lifted her head, offering him a shy smile. Dark eyes, slightly flushed cheeks, a rosebud of a mouth…

Claw's mind went blank.

FIVE

Franny found herself at the table beside Iva. "So, is he here? Your unsuitable match?" Franny whispered.

Iva shook her head. "I don't think so. This isn't his sort of thing. But don't worry about me. Let's find the perfect match for you. Let's see…tiny dick, tiny dick, probably hasn't been laid in years, tiny dick, won't know what to do with it…"

"Dick size isn't everything!" Franny protested.

Iva regarded her. "No, but you are looking for someone who can satisfy you, right? Trust me, big dicks are better. Ooh, here we go…three contenders. The rich boy, the farm boy, and Mr Muscles. You want the muscles for sure. That guy is hung!"

"Iva!" Franny hissed, ducking her head when Mr Muscles appeared to not only have heard her, but was looking their way. "I'm not just looking for a hookup. I'd actually like to meet someone I have a chance of love with."

"So invite him over and talk to him for a bit. We don't have to go back to the farm until midnight. You have time to talk before you pin him to the table and ride him." She paused. "I've caught his eye, he's coming over…yes! Oh, horses got nothing on this guy. You're in for a good night, Franny. Get an orgasm for me, while you're at it."

Franny felt her cheeks grow hot. If he'd heard any of that, she was never going to be able to look him in the eye, let alone talk to him. At least he wouldn't be able to catch her staring at his equipment, enormous or otherwise, now it was hidden under the table.

He spoke first. "Hi."

It took her an agonisingly long moment to get her tongue to cooperate. "Um, hello. I'm Franny. Frangipani, actually, but everyone calls me Franny."

He seemed to be just as nervous as she was. "I'm Claw. Just…Claw." He held out his hand – completely without claws, thankfully – for her to shake.

His hand engulfed hers, yet he shook hers gently. A point in his favour.

"Why are you here?" he asked.

Well, that was blunt. And yet, so vague she couldn't be sure what he meant. Here in this pub? Here in the Colony? Here in the Altan System? Or just here at this matchmaking thing?

She took a deep breath, and decided honesty would be best.

"I signed up for the Colony because my mother wanted me to. There was nothing left for me on Earth and this was a new future, a new start with more opportunities than I had at home. And

I'm here in this pub…well, that's complicated, I guess. I've been working so hard, I can't remember the last time I went to a pub, or met someone, and when I heard about this dating event, I thought…I thought that this was my chance, you know? To meet someone. Maybe…to have what my mother never managed to find back on Earth. Love, family, partnership. But all that comes later. It starts with…a date."

He was staring at her, like she'd grown two heads or something. She wasn't the alien. He was, wasn't he? He didn't look any different from her. Just a normal Human, with impressive muscles.

He swallowed and seemed to remember that staring was rude. "So you…just volunteered, and they accepted you?"

Franny bobbed her head. "Of course. I mean, the other girls at the farm signed up, too. Pretty much all of us are here. Good thing, too – there are a lot of guys here. Equal numbers, though, seeing as everyone's paired off." She took another breath. Time to get him talking. "So, why are you here?"

SIX

Oh, stars. He should have come up with something to say, but his mind was just blank. He'd never found a girl so mesmerising in his life. And honest. He had no doubt that everything she'd just blurted out, her reasons for being here, were absolutely the truth.

Could it really be as easy as a bunch of

farm girls had heard about the event, and taken all the female places before the Mer girls had tried to sign up?

Which meant the girl in front of him, the one with the enchanting eyes, deserved honesty from him, too.

"My friend wanted me to come," he said.

She nodded. "So you're a good friend? Helping out a mate, who's looking for love?"

He wanted to nod, to take the compliment he didn't deserve. He wanted to stare into those eyes and talk to her all night. Maybe even kiss her, if she was willing.

But he couldn't bring himself to lie to her.

"I'm…I need to leave early, to get to

work. It was nice meeting you," he said, rising to his feet.

Her lovely eyes widened. "But we only just met. The event isn't over yet."

He grimaced. "Sorry, but bread doesn't bake itself. And if I don't get the dough rising early enough, tomorrow morning I'll have angry customers banging down my door."

It took every bit of his self control to turn away from her, and walk out the door.

SEVEN

Well, that was rude. Mr Muscles was definitely not relationship material, Franny told himself. Pity. Especially with all those muscles and hadn't he said he worked in a bakery?

"Go after him!" Iva hissed.

Franny started to shake her head. No way was she following some rude baker out into the street of an unfamiliar city.

"Now, you idiot!" Iva seized the back of Franny's chair and yanked it, so she had no choice but to stand up or fall on the floor.

This was insane. She shouldn't do this.

But her feet refused to listen, breaking into a run as she followed Claw out of the pub.

EIGHT

"Do you need some help?"

She just appeared in front of him, like magic. She must have followed him out of the pub.

"I'm a fully qualified baker and pastry chef. I've spent the last year working on a farm, hoping we'd finally harvest enough grain for flour so I could make bread. Seriously, I will do half the prep work for your bakery, just for a bite of something that isn't a ration bar when I'm done."

"You're hired." The words were out of his mouth before he'd really thought them through. He barely knew this girl. He barely knew what he was doing in the bakery. And with this Intergalactic Dating Agency turning out to be as ordinary and legal as, well, bread, he shouldn't even be thinking of spending more time with her.

"So, what's your specialty?" she asked as they climbed onto a skimmer.

"My what?"

"Your specialty. Every baker and pastry chef has a signature dish. I have three. Tiger rolls, profiteroles and croissants, because I wasn't sure whether I wanted to work in a bakery, a patisserie or a restaurant, so that gave me something impressive for all three."

Stars. This was even worse an idea than he'd thought. The moment she saw his baking skills, she was going to laugh herself sick. Worse, he didn't even know what two of those things were.

"What in the galaxy is a tiger roll?" he asked.

She laughed. "It was my mother's favourite. The bread is made with a rice flour paste on top, which cracks when it bakes, giving it tiger stripes. You can make it as a loaf or rolls, but the hardest part is the paste. Too thin and it burns, so you just get little leopard spots that aren't very impressive, but too thick and you weigh down the rolls, so they don't rise properly. Done well, they turn out like round rolls, but with the top of them all done in crispy tiger stripes."

He wasn't going to ask about the profit-a-whatsits. He'd look them up later, if he dared.

The tiger rolls didn't sound impossible, though. He even had some rice flour, though he hadn't decided what he wanted to do with it yet. He'd initially considered using it for gluten free bread, but the gluten free flour from the synthesiser was easier to work with, and the supply never ran out. Well, if he was really desperate, he could set the food synthesiser to make the entire gluten free loaf, but the texture wasn't quite right and there was the telltale metallic aftertaste, which he could eliminate when he used synthesised flour and baked like it was natural. Something in the baking process neutralised the artificial nature of the flour and it became actual food instead of a machine's imitation.

He couldn't remember the difference being so pronounced back on Alba, but then the synthesisers had all been controlled by the Central Intelligence, a system-wide AI that held all Titan information and constantly learned from it. The AI they'd trusted until it went mad and turned all the robots against the population – starting with the President. Until that day, he'd believed rogue AIs that turned on their makers only existed in ancient science fiction.

Now, it wasn't just rogue AIs but all

AIs that were relegated to science fiction, or the history books. There would never be another Central Intelligence. Not while a Titan still lived and breathed.

"The Bear Claw Bakery," Franny read, staring at the shopfront. "Wow, is this yours?"

Claw nodded.

"Why did you call it that?"

"Because bear claws are my signature dish, and because…" He flexed his fingers, feeling the strange tingling that preceded a shift, before he was flexing his mighty paws instead.

"Oh my God! Can I touch them?" Without waiting for his permission, she reached out to stroke the back of his paw, before running her fingers lightly over his claws then down his furless palms. "That's really you. You're…an alien, aren't you?"

"I'm a Titan," Claw corrected. "And I can change all of me, not just my hands."

"Into what?" she breathed.

Most Humans were terrified by Titan abilities, but Franny just looked fascinated.

"I'm a bear shifter. I turn into a Kodiak bear when I want to."

"Could you do it here, now?"

"Yes, but I'd have to take all my clothes off, as my bear form is considerably bigger. And…I'm not sure about you, but we've only just met, and I have to admit, I've never gotten naked on a first date." He probably shouldn't have said that. Maybe he should have said girls were tearing his clothes off every first date. But it would be a lie.

Franny nodded. "Right. Not to mention you might not fit on the scooter as a bear. Or worse, it might fall out of the air under the weight."

Scooter? Perhaps she meant the skimmer. Maybe that's what they'd called them on Earth.

She dismounted and stood staring raptly up at the bakery sign, like she was terribly impressed by it. "You won't believe how long I've waited for this moment. I'm going to bake my first loaf of bread in space!"

How could he say no to that? Claw palmed open the door, and ushered her inside.

NINE

"What do you want me to do first?" Franny asked, pushing up her sleeves. If she'd known she'd be in a bakery tonight, she would have picked one of the sleeveless dresses.

"Put on an apron," Claw said, tossing one to her. "Then wash your hands."

When her sanitised hands were dry,

she found him looking at her expectantly.

"What would you do first?" he asked.

Ah, a test. Fair enough. "I'd mix up the bread dough, and put it somewhere to rise."

"I usually do the croissants first."

Thoughtfully, Franny nodded. Mum had always prepped the croissant dough in the morning, so they could work on those after the bread dough. "Is the dough in the freezer, ready for tourrage, or do we need to mix that up first?"

Claw nodded at one of the high shelves. "I set it to thaw before I left for the pub." He brought the bowl down, for which she was grateful. She'd have needed a ladder, or at least a chair to reach it.

It was the perfect temperature. He really hadn't been blowing her off in the pub – he'd needed to get back here on time.

"And the butter?" she asked.

"I'll get it." He disappeared behind a door that presumably led to the cool room, returning a moment later with a metal bowl full of what looked like butter. But it wasn't.

"I said butter," she said.

Claw grimaced. "Yeah, we're out. Something happened to the Colony's dairy herd – some sort of illness – and they all had to be euthanised. So until a new herd of cows is old enough to give milk…this is the best we have. I made it fresh last night."

"You…made it?" Now she couldn't

help but stare at him, trying to work out how. The only thing she could think of was… "Do alien males lactate?"

He exploded into laughter. "Stars, no. At least, not any of the guys I've met. Maybe there is some Titan that does, but not one I know of. This stuff's made with powdered milk, oil, water and salt. Oh, and a bit of colouring, or it'd be white, not yellow."

Franny eyed it with suspicion. "Let me guess…it's even more temperature sensitive than real butter? Does it break easily?"

"Like you wouldn't believe. It needs a strong, soft touch."

That explained the muscles, then. Coupled with those big hands…

"How about you do the croissants,

while I get started on the bread? How much should I prepare?” Franny asked, heading for the sacks of flour stacked up along the wall.

“Those have to last us all week. I won’t get another delivery until next Friday. But Saturdays are my busiest day, so you could probably use two sacks tonight, because I’ll only need one on the weekdays.”

She eyed the sacks. “Are you sure? We’d go through all of them on a Friday night for Mum’s bakery back home, and we lived in a small farming town. This is a big city. If I bake it, they’ll sell. Can’t you just order more flour for tomorrow?”

Claw shook his head. “This is all the flour I’ve been allocated. My portion of the harvest. Even if I wanted to order more, there simply isn't any. The first wheat crops didn't do too well in New Hope's soil, so it took until this harvest before I could have wheat flour at all. I've had to use the food synthesiser more than I care to admit."

So it wasn't just Star Farm that had struggled to pull in a decent harvest. There were other farms in the Colony. Then his words sank in. "What's a food synthesiser?"

Claw waved at a blocky machine that looked like a coffee maker. "This. Standard issue on Titan spacecraft. It's programmed to make synthetic food that the company that makes them says is almost indistinguishable from the real thing. It has all the nutrients of normal food, sure, and it's made up of most of the same things, but the taste is…lacking. And it has a bad aftertaste."

Wow. These aliens really were more advanced than Humans. She'd never heard of such a thing before. "Can it make me a strawberry tart?" It was the one thing she'd loved most, and she hadn't had one in forever.

"It can make something that will look like a strawberry tart…but I can make you a real one," Claw said.

"You have real strawberries?" she cried, unable to help herself.

Claw opened the door of the cool room and pointed. There was a whole shelf of strawberry punnets. Her mouth watered, and she had to close it quickly before she drooled down the front of her apron. Real strawberries. She was in heaven.

She rubbed her hands together. "Right, let's get started, then. The sooner we get the bread and croissants done, the sooner we can take a coffee break."

So they did.

TEN

Sinking her fingers into the bowl of flour was like coming home, Franny thought as she worked the dough until it took on a life of its own and began to resist. Then she set that batch aside, and moved onto the next bowl.

She forgot about the muscled man she'd followed here. The one she was supposed to be considering as a prospective partner. Her thoughts were filled with the smell of yeast, the stretch of the dough beneath her fingers, the fug of flour that seemed to coat her tongue even when she kept her mouth closed, the flumping sound as she emptied the last sack into her bowl, and the soft froth of the yeast in its bath of warm water before she emptied it into the final bowl of flour.

All too soon, she was done. More than a dozen bowls queued on the counter, slowing puffing up with pride that they were well on their way to becoming more than flour and water and yeast. They would be the first loaves of bread Franny baked in space, so perhaps their pride was not misplaced.

"How are you doing?"

She'd forgotten all about the massive man on the other side of the kitchen. But now he had her attention, she couldn't seem to take her eyes off him. His muscles bulged as he rolled the pastry paper thin, the final stage before cutting it to be rolled up into croissants.

She moved to his side, wanting to touch, but she didn't dare. "Want me to start cutting?" she asked, picking up a knife.

"If you want."

What she wanted was to watch him lean over the counter, pressing down on the dough so that his arm muscles threatened to tear through his shirt. The rolling pin had to be made of titanium not to break under such power.

She tore her eyes away from him long enough to slice the pastry, before she dared to feast her eyes on him again. She didn't need to see the pastry to know she was shaping it into perfect croissants. She'd been doing this since primary school, and she could definitely do it with her eyes closed. Or otherwise occupied.

She filled tray after tray with the rolls of pastry that, once proven and glazed and baked, would become croissants, chasing Claw down the counter with agonising slowness as he rolled out sheet after sheet for her, until there were none left.

Then, her fingers tangled with his as they reached for the same slice of pastry.

Laughter and mumbled apologies

tumbled one over the other, before he selected a piece at the other end of the sheet.

His hands were deft and sure, but not as quick as hers. Looking at the tray of finished crescents, she was hard pressed to pick which ones were hers and which ones were his.

"Do you need help with the bread?" he asked.

Franny shook her head slowly. "All done." She pointed at the bowls.

"Fuck me…it's not even midnight yet!" he exclaimed.

She regarded him thoughtfully. Actually, she thought she'd like to do that very much.

ELEVEN

"You must be an angel," Claw whispered as he set the last tray of croissants on the shelf to prove.

Franny shook her head. "Nope. Definitely Human. And a baker, though I'm a bit rusty. It's been a while."

"You're amazing." The next thing he knew, he was kissing her.

And she was kissing him back.

Clothes and flour flew. Aprons were tossed aside. A knife went clattering to the floor, but Claw was too busy lifting her up onto the counter so he could keep kissing her while his hands explored her body. Her legs wrapped around his hips, pulling him closer.

They came together like asteroids colliding, not caring about the damage around them when all they wanted was to be as close as two people could be.

Claw barely had the wits to roll on a condom before he was inside her, urged on by her sweet cries for more, yes, just like that, oh, harder, please…

His orgasm came fast and hard, hot on the heels of hers, for she was still clenched around him as if she meant to keep him.

"Stars, yes!" he shouted. He'd never had sex this good. Not ever. A beautiful baker who'd just given him the best orgasm of his life.

He was in love.

TWELVE

She could have ridden Claw's cock all night. She definitely wanted to. But her ride home to the farm would be waiting outside the pub at midnight, and Franny didn't know what would happen if she was late. Nothing good, anyway.

So she reluctantly untangled herself from Claw's deliciously muscled body, moaning a little at the loss of his cock, before dragging her clothes back on and running out the door, shoes in hand.

The others were just climbing into an aircar when she arrived at the pub, so she hurried to join them, hoping no one would notice she'd been gone.

"What did I tell you? Big cocks are the best, aren't they?"

Franny glanced behind her to find Iva grinning.

"Maybe," Franny bit out, before pressing her lips together. She was still riding her orgasm high. In fact, if she closed her eyes, she could almost feel him still inside her, filling her more completely than she'd ever thought possible. Big? No, the alien bear shifter baker was bloody massive.

And amazing.

She should have been talking to as many men as possible, trying to find her perfect match. Not spending hours doing bakery prep, before banging the baker in the middle of his kitchen.

But…God, it had been good.

"I bet he'll come back to the Cantina to see you again next week," Iva whispered.

Oh, if only.

But she'd go back next week, in the hope of seeing him again.

And if she didn't…perhaps she could spend an evening doing what she was supposed to be doing, instead of bloody baking.

What would her mother say if she knew Franny had had sex in a bakery kitchen? Nothing good, that's for sure.

72

THIRTEEN

"You're getting better every day, Claw!"

"I think these are your best yet!"

Any other day, the stream of customer compliments would have set him aglow with pride, but Claw couldn't seem to concentrate. All he could think of was her, and how incredible she'd felt in his arms last night.

He had to see her again.

It was almost like he was in love, which, aside from the occasional orgasm-induced insane declaration, couldn't possibly be the case. He'd only met her yesterday, for stars' sake, and he knew next to nothing about her.

Except that she was sweet and beautiful, made both bread and pastries like the goddess of bakeries, possessed the most heavenly pussy he'd ever had the honour to enter, she worked on a farm, and by some miracle was still single.

Word must have spread about his unusually good bread today, because he'd sold out of everything well before noon. But after Claw closed the shop, instead of going to sleep like a sensible man, he went hunting.

For her.

FOURTEEN

After several hours of searching the networks for something, anything, to help him find Miss Frangipani, Franny to her friends, which he hoped he might become, if not more…Claw growled and tossed his tablet across the room. Luckily, it hit the couch instead of smashing against the wall, so he didn't have to go out and get a new one, but not even a new tablet would help when there wasn't anything about her in the Colony network.

If they had a Central Intelligence, like the one on Tito, he'd have only had to ask the AI, which would have told him everything he needed to know. He almost wished the Colony had its own AI. Not as omnipotent as the Central Intelligence, of course, but omnipresent enough to be able to help.

Finally, he fell asleep, only to wake from an uneasy doze with the wonderful thought that she'd surely return to the bakery tonight.

Only…she didn't. Not that night, or the next night, or the night after that.

It was like he'd imagined her.

Except…she'd left her underwear behind. He'd found the pair of knickers under one of the counters this morning, dusted with flour but still loaded with her intoxicating scent.

The first night, he'd slept with it beneath his pillow, her scent driving him mad until he had to take himself in hand. Not once, but twice, before he could sleep.

The next night, it was three times. Then four.

Until Friday night rolled around again and the next Intergalactic Dating Agency speed dating event at the One Shot Cantina.

He called Fang and Talon, asking if they'd come with him, expecting them to refuse. But they were both as eager as he was to return to the Cantina, so he found no support there. In fact, the only support they offered was to flank him as he walked into the pub, eagerly scanning the patrons for a glimpse of his goddess.

Only to realise he'd forgotten the gift he'd baked specially for her that morning.

FIFTEEN

Franny had barely sat down at the pub table before her eyes met his. Only Claw didn't look happy to see her.

All the more reason she should pay attention to the other men present, instead of him, she told herself as he slumped into the seat across from her.

"I made you a present," he began.

Yet his open hands were empty.

"I spent hours making sure it was perfect. The best ingredients. Fresh, not synthesised. I even put it on one of the presentation platters we use for cakes, and then carefully boxed it up…" He buried his head in his hands. "Only I left the box in the cool room."

Before she could think, Franny was on her feet. "Let's go to your bakery, then."

Alarm bells clanged in her head. She was supposed to be searching for her perfect mate, talking to as many people as possible, not sneaking out with her one night stand from last week.

"Really?" Those were definitely puppy dog eyes, and there was no way Franny could resist them.

She took his hand. "Yeah. I've been

dreaming about getting my hands on your pastry all week."

Oh God, that sounded awful.

But it made him grin, and damn, did he have a gorgeous smile. "You've been in my thoughts a lot since last week, too."

When they were pressed together on a skimmer, heading for the bakery, he asked, "So, what have you been doing all week?"

"The usual stuff. Farming. Seeding the new fields, hoping we'll have a decent wheat crop this time, come harvest, so I have flour to work with. It's all work, from dawn until dusk, and at the end of the day, I'm too tired to do anything else except fall into bed and the next thing I know, it's morning. Time to start work again."

"Which farm do you work at?" he asked.

"Star Farm. We all do — all the girls at the One Shot Cantina tonight. We live and breathe agriculture, even when we don't want to, because that's all there is until the farm's properly established and productive."

"I never heard of Star Farm. Then again, I only know the farms I've received produce from. If you're farming wheat and there isn't enough flour for you to bake with, I don't imagine there'd be any of your flour in my deliveries. Where in the Ag Dome is it? What level?"

"There's an entire dome devoted to agriculture? So that's where you get your flour from. We're in the Nyx Dome, if you know that one."

"My friends Talon and Fang live there. Originally, I had an apartment there, too, but when you run a bakery, it's so much easier living above the shop, so when the bakery opened, I moved here."

Franny found herself nodding. "Yeah, that's what Mum said, too. She never would have coped as a single mum if she'd had to leave the house to work. As it was, she could put me to bed for the night, and go downstairs to work in the bakery, with a baby monitor on the bench in case I woke up. When I grew up, we still kept the baby monitor, but we switched out the units, so the receiver was in the kitchen, and the baby unit was on the counter in the shop, so we could hear if someone came in." She sighed. "I wonder what happened to it. Probably went in the bin, with everything else."

"Wouldn't your mother still be using it? It sounds quite ingenious," Claw said.

Franny swallowed. Part of her wanted to brush off the question and just agree with him, but something made her want to tell him the truth. "If she was still alive and baking, I imagine she would, but…right about the time I signed up for the Farm Stars program, she lost the shop. Not through any fault of her own, either. You see, I grew up being told my father left when I was a baby, and that's why I never knew him…but it turned out he was one of the farmers outside of town, and he was married. He owned the building we lived in – it was empty, inherited from family from when one of his grandparents ran a shop in town — and he let Mum run her business rent free from it. He promised he'd sign it over to me when I was eighteen, which is why Mum insisted I start an apprenticeship with her instead of going to boarding school like Rue and the other girls. So I could take over my inheritance, when the time came." A bitter laugh escaped her lips before she could stop it.

"What happened?" Claw asked, his arms tightening around her in what felt almost like a hug.

"His wife found out he was cheating on her — not with Mum, someone else this time — and filed for divorce. So he declared bankruptcy, and a bunch of lawyers took everything. The bakery, our apartment, his farm. Then one morning I found Mum unconscious in the kitchen. I called an ambulance, they took her to hospital…and that's when we found out it wasn't just the stress of losing the bakery, but cancer. The late stage, not long to live kind."

Claw swore. "I'm so sorry for your loss. I had no idea."

Franny shrugged. "She pushed me to join the Farm Stars program. She wanted to know that I'd have a future. One my unfaithful arse of a father couldn't ruin for me. I wasn't going to deny my mother her dying wish, so I signed up, worked hard on all the training they gave us, hoping that when we'd terraformed Elysium, I'd be able to start a bakery here in the Colony. Or at least work for someone who had. Having worked with the farmers, I'd have all the right contacts for negotiating supply contracts, when the time came." She laughed softly. "Mum actually had a business degree. She met my dad while they were at uni together. One night was all it took…and by the time she saw him again, he was married to someone else. So, now you know. I'm the bastard daughter of a failed business student turned baker, and an unfaithful farmer who liked to fuck anything that moved."

She kept her eyes down on the road beneath the skimmer, blinking back angry tears. She would not cry over that arsehole. "So, what were your parents like? All happy alien families, with the standard two kids and a dog?"

He chuckled. "Something like that. They both had boring government jobs back on Tito, which paid okay, if not well, so when I was in high school, I took on a weekend job at the local bakery. My parents wanted me to aim high, but they wanted me to study something that was useful, so I went to university to study law. Not the flashy kind you see in historical dramas, but contract law. Preparing and assessing laws and contracts." He hesitated, like he wanted to add something else, then decided against it. "But when I moved to the Colony, I wanted to do something simpler. So I started a bakery."

"And now you're the only baker in the Colony, aren't you?"

"Well, except for you. I'm the only practicing one, and as you've already seen, I need a lot more practice before I'm anywhere near as good as you. It doesn't help that I have to keep looking up recipes on the network, because I don't remember them, or I can't get the ingredients I need and I have to substitute them for something else, or worse, synthesise them." She felt him shudder.

"What do your parents think of you running a bakery?" she asked.

"I don't know. They didn't make it off Tito. The building they worked in was destroyed in one of the first robot attacks, when the Central Intelligence killed the President. I was in orbit, taking some time off, or I might have died with them. As it was, we just watched in horror until Fang rustled up a few of his ships to go down to the surface to pick up refugees and supplies. They landed on Talon's family's farm, so they all made it out. They're in the Ag Dome here, actually. I get shipments of fruit from them sometimes."

Now it was her turn to offer sympathies. "I'm sorry, Claw. I had no idea. I guess when I heard we were sharing the Colony with aliens, I thought more about how excited I was to meet them than why they were here. So that's why you went to war for the Altan System. You're all refugees with nowhere to go."

"No different to any of the Humans. I understand Earth is still habitable, but

Exodus, the space station your *Genesis* was docked at, suffered irreparable damage in the terrorist attack that destroyed your space elevator. You had no choice but to board the *Genesis* and come here."

Whatever he'd heard about Humans, that wasn't right at all. "No, the *Genesis* is a colony ship. We signed up for the Farm Stars program to join the Colony. To terraform Elysium. I chose to come here. I went into stasis and woke up here, exactly like I was supposed to. If there were any changes to the plan, it was because we had to share the Altan System with aliens." Where had he heard such terrible things? Terrorists destroying Exodus? That would be catastrophic for Earth's shipbuilding industry, and if the space elevator was gone, too, that would isolate Earth from the rest of the system.

His arms closed around her waist as he pressed his lips to her neck. "I bet you never thought you'd be so close to an alien, you'd be sharing a skimmer with him."

Now he was pressed against her, she couldn't help but feel the massive bulge at her back. Now all she could think about was getting him inside the bakery, so she could free his cock and ride it until she screamed.

Who cared about stars and space elevators and shipyards when she had a hot alien right here?

SIXTEEN

He led the way into the bakery, suddenly self conscious. Would his best efforts be good enough for her? Now she knew he wasn't really a qualified baker, but as there hadn't been anyone else who wanted to run the place, the Colony Administration had allowed him to do it…

Stars, what if she hated it?

He really was overthinking this. If she hated it, then he'd offer to make her something else. Anything else.

He palmed open the cool room door, and ventured inside.

The box was exactly where he'd left it.

If he'd known she'd be eating it here, he would have plated it properly. Added a garnish. Done everything he could to make his offering look irresistible.

But she was out there waiting now, and he didn't have any plates in here. The box would just have to do.

He existed the cool room in a cloud of condensation, clutching the box in both hands. He laid it before her on the bench with a flourish, then bowed low. "Your gift, my lady."

At least she had the good grace to laugh. Perhaps she'd forgiven him for the truly horrible conversation on the skimmer. The tragic deaths of your parents weren't something you were supposed to discuss on a second date.

Slowly, she lifted the lid.

Her joyful smile made every moment worth it.

"Is it real?" she breathed.

He nodded. "Fresh strawberries from Eden, the last of the real butter, flour from the Ag Dome, sugar from the first sugarcane crop grown here, also from the Ag Dome, eggs from some new kind of chicken Eden are calling a Chicken Salad, the stars only know why, and water from….well, it comes from under the planet's surface, where it's been frozen for thousands if not millions of years. So maybe not fresh, but…definitely locally sourced and as pure as you'll find anywhere in the Colony."

She couldn't stop staring. "And you made it?"

"In the early hours of this morning. Yes."

"I haven't had one of these since the day my mother collapsed. I was making them when I heard her fall, and I don't even remember putting the half-done tray in the cool room, but I must have, because when I got back from the hospital, I didn't have any energy to cook dinner, and they were just there and…I think I ate four of them before I had to stop or I'd be sick. We lost the bakery soon after that, so I never had the chance to make them again. I swore they'd be the first thing I made when I had my own bakery in space."

Stars. He should have made her something else instead. Anything but a strawberry tart.

She reached into the box, cradling the cake carefully in her fingers, before taking a bite.

Claw held his breath.

She closed her eyes, hesitating a moment before starting to chew. She didn't say a word until she swallowed. Only then did she open her eyes.

"Was it all right?" he asked.

"This is the best alien strawberry tart I've ever tasted," she said.

He allowed himself to smile. She liked

it!

"What sort of sugar did you use?" she continued.

"Uh, the ordinary kind," he said.

"And you blind baked them with weights?"

"Of…of course."

Stars. She did hate it, if she thought he'd baked it wrong.

"Do you want to know how to make them even better?" Franny asked.

He'd take any help she could give him. He nodded, feeling like a bobble head.

"Swap the normal sugar for icing sugar. Powdered sugar, confectioner's sugar…whatever you call it. That stuff. It'll make the tart casing less crumbly, more melt in your mouth. And you can skip the blind baking, because you won't need weights if you use an aerated baking tray…and perforated tart moulds. That was Mum's secret to the perfect tart casing." She grinned. "If you've got everything we need, I could show you, if you like?"

The bobble-headed baker nodded again.

"You get everything out, while I finish this delicious tart," she said, and took another bite.

SEVENTEEN

Three times they stopped in the middle of baking, so he could have his way with her. Or so she could have her way with him, Claw wasn't sure.

The first time, he'd been unable to stop staring at her as she bent over the bench, her skirt riding up so high he could see… "You're not wearing any underwear!"

She'd shot him an impish grin. "I figure after losing them last week, what was the point of wearing any tonight? Less clothes to get in the way when you're of a mind to give me more of that mighty cock of yours."

"You mean you're trying to distract me?"

Franny rolled her eyes, before hiking her skirt up to her waist, baring her bottom and the glistening wetness he wanted more than anything. "I'm trying to tell you I want to feel your cock deep inside me. I figure I'll give you about five more minutes before I tear your apron off you, climb you like a tree, and ride your cock like the randiest monkey you ever saw."

In five seconds, he was inside her, and by five minutes, he had her screaming through her first orgasm of the night. But definitely not the last.

The last time, she'd come on his tongue, tasting sweeter than the frosting he'd licked off her. And the sound of her screaming his name…bliss. He'd be dreaming about her for weeks.

His cock would be aching for days, too, most likely, with the workout she'd given him. She was already tight, but when she came, she squeezed him so hard, he almost came with her, every time. It took every bit of willpower he had not to finish early, to give her as much pleasure as he could.

Before she'd left, they'd shared a strawberry tart. One of the ones she'd made, with the powdered sugar and the perforated whatever they weres, which were a thousand times better than any tart he'd ever baked. He was man enough to admit it, too.

But she'd just smiled, like she already knew.

All through the night, as Claw finished baking everything he needed to fill the bakery shelves the next morning, his thoughts were on Franny.

Talon and Fang had joked about finding their fated mates at the Intergalactic Dating Agency, never believing that any of them would get lucky at the Cantina. Yet last night, both of them had gravitated toward girls they were definitely smitten with, while he…

Stars, she was perfect. Everything he

ever wanted in a woman, but didn't know. Amazing in bed – not that they'd ever actually made it to bed – and amazing in the kitchen, in every way possible. So much energy and positivity, despite everything that had happened to her, and when she smiled at him…

Yep, there it went again. His cock went rock hard as his heart melted.

Either she was his fated mate, or he was hopelessly in love with Miss Frangipani of Star Farm. Maybe even both.

EIGHTEEN

It wasn't until Claw closed the bakery for the day – yet another day full of compliments for Franny's divine cooking – that he had time to call Allie.

"One sec…I'm knee deep in you don't want to know what and if I don't get this shut off, it's going to be flooding down the street. Give me five minutes, and I'll call you back, Orson."

He grinned, and waited. It was hard to imagine Allie as just a plumber, what with everything she'd done during the war and the peace negotiations, but he could hardly talk. He was just a barely trained baker.

Fifteen minutes passed before Allie called back. "Tell me you have good news, or I'm going to tell you about my morning."

Claw laughed. "Actually, I do have good news. That Intergalactic Dating Agency you wanted me to investigate? You've got nothing to worry about. Your girls couldn't get spaces at the event because they're all taken by women from a female farming collective. One of them saw the event, and they all signed up.

They're all Earth girls, actual colonists, even though most of the rest of the Humans aboard the *Genesis* weren't, and there's not a whiff of coercion or anything about them. They're genuinely looking for love." With a heavy dollop of sex, he thought but didn't say, rubbing his groin through his pants.

"I don't know of any female farming collective in the Colony," Allie said.

Well, she couldn't know everything, could she? "Something about stars…Star Farm, in the Nyx Dome. Maybe that's why you haven't heard of them, because they're not in the Ag Dome like the rest of the Colony farms."

"Orson, there are farms in every dome in the Colony, not just the Ag Dome. Different crops and creatures prefer different climates, and we're trying to feed a whole city here. But Star Farm? That's not a collective. That's a school. With children. They were kept in stasis at the request of their head teacher, a woman named Donna, until they could be awoken in the Colony, in an enclosed environment. They're child migrants with no family back on Earth, so they're cloistered in Star Farm, learning how to farm here, under this system's sun, until they're all legal adults. When they're old enough, then they can be integrated into the community, but there's just so much…the girls were put into stasis early, before the *Genesis* was even completed. They know nothing of the destruction of Exodus, or Earth's space elevator, or even the war between

Humans and Titans here. I don't envy the person who gets to give them that history lesson, when the time comes."

"But…they didn't look like children…"

"Well, it's been a few years. Maybe some of them have grown. They couldn't be old enough to go to a pub, though. They shouldn't even have left the farm. Maybe you met Donna, their head teacher. Not that I remember any other teachers. Just her. If there were any other teachers, they stayed asleep, along with the children. It must have been Donna you talked to. Because the children aren't allowed to leave Star Farm."

Claw didn't know what to say. She'd said her name was Franny, not Donna. She'd said she and all the other girls worked on the farm. Nothing about teachers or children or…oh, stars.

She hadn't known about the Exodus or the space elevator.

Maybe Allie was right.

Which meant…

He couldn't possibly be a paedophile! He wasn't attracted to children at all, except in the way normal adults wanted to protect them.

"Look, I know it's a big ask, but could you possibly go back the Cantina next week, and talk to the same woman you did last week? Ask her for her name. I'm sure it'll be Donna. And then…maybe talk to some of the others. Find out where they're from. Because if they're all from Star Farm…"

Then someone's pimping out children,

Claw finished for her grimly.

"Well, let's just say that we can tear up the peace treaty if those girls are roaming around. It'll mean war. Which is why you have to tell me you're wrong."

Wonderful. War and child molesting.

"Oh, I'll be there, all right. I'll get all your answers and more next week," Claw promised her.

Only when he'd ended the call did he realise that he wasn't the only one who'd fallen for the girls' charms. Both Talon and Fang had been smitten, too.

He swore. He had to call them, before they did something stupid.

NINETEEN

Franny was thoroughly sick of farming. If she never had to fill a seeder again, she would die happy. Admittedly, she'd felt this way before she'd seen any of the rest of the Colony, but it grated even more now that she knew she could be in Claw's bakery right now, doing things she was actually good at, instead of planting wheat or potatoes or cabbage or whatever crops were supposed to grow in this field.

Rue would know. She actually liked farming, and she paid attention to the farm more than the people around her.

"So what are we growing here again?" Franny asked.

For a moment, she didn't think Rue had heard her. Then Rue said, "Rats," half under her breath, kicking at the soil, before she met Franny's gaze. "What?"

Franny repeated her question, and Franny frowned.

"Another wheat varietal. That's the fourth one this month. They're trying to find one that will grow in the light of a red dwarf sun, so we can use it to terraform Elysium. We haven't had a decent harvest from any of the new breeds yet, and I think they're starting to get desperate. But maybe it's not the wheat to blame. Maybe it's the rats."

Franny reared back, horrified. "There are rats here? In this brand new city, halfway across the galaxy from home? How is that even possible?"

Rue shrugged. "Same way rats got everywhere, I guess. On the ships that carried the colonists."

"Well, are we putting down poison? Buying a cat? Or one of those little dogs that kind of looks like a rat?" If they weren't doing something, no way was she sleeping in here. Not if there were rats. She'd sneak out to Claw's place and ask if she could stay with him.

"Donna hired a rat catcher to deal

with them. I haven't seen any live ones since then," Rue said.

Franny breathed a sigh of relief. "So they're gone, then?"

"Maybe."

"Do you still miss home?" The question hung in the air, heavy as humidity.

"My home's gone. So's yours," Rue said, marching up the next row with the seeder.

"Yes, but just because they're gone, doesn't mean you don't miss them. Don't you…"

"The sooner we get a good wheat crop, the sooner you'll have flour to start baking again. I'll have a farm. You'll have a bakery. You can't change the past, no matter how much you want to, and the people…the people we wish were still there, at the home we no longer have, they'd want us to be planning for the future, not mourning the past. They'd want us to be happy instead of miserable. Wouldn't your mum want that?"

"Yeah, she would."

"What's the first thing you're going to bake, when you get your bakery?" Rue asked.

"Strawberry tarts," Franny said, ducking her head to hide her smile. Claw had given her one to take home, and it had looked so good, she'd eaten it before she arrived back at the Cantina. It had been years since she'd made one, but some things you didn't forget.

Of course, knowing there was other food in the Colony made eating ration bars here on the farm so much harder.

"What's the first thing you're going to plant when you get your own farm?" Franny asked. They'd played this game so many times, she could have answered for her, but then it wouldn't be the same.

"Grape vines," Rue said. "And why are we doing this?"

Together, they said, "Building a better world, for the good of the Colony."

"And for us," Rue added this time. "Because we deserve to be happy, too."

"Are you sure?"

"Positive."

They continued working in silence, but Franny couldn't help turning it all over in her head, just as the seeder turned the soil behind whatever it was planting.

Going to the pub once a week for the

dating events was supposed to be helping her find happiness, or at least someone who made her happy. Was it wrong to pin all her hopes on Claw? She adored working in his bakery – the only bakery in the Colony, no less, at least until the wheat yield improved – and she was unashamedly in love with his cock and the things he could do with it. The rest of him was pretty hot, too, and they worked well together…

Next Friday, she was going to tell him she wanted to date him. That she was interested in more than meeting once a week at the pub, before sneaking off to his bakery. Maybe even spending the whole night, if Donna didn't throw her in solitary for daring to spend a night away from the farm.

Yes. She wanted Claw, not some random man she hadn't yet met. She was willing to take a chance on happiness with him.

And she knew exactly how she wanted to paint her nails for Friday.

TWENTY

Franny was drumming her nails on the table when Claw arrived, later than he would have liked. He'd considered not coming, but he had to see her again, if only to know the truth. If he was really as horrible a person as he thought.

But he couldn't take his eyes off those ruby red nails. Stars, he wanted her to dig them into his back or his butt as he thrust deep between her thighs, until she screamed for joy.

He couldn't. He shouldn't have done it. No matter how much he wanted to, it was wrong.

Then he sat down, and saw them clearly. "They're strawberries! You've painted your nails like little strawberries! With the seeds and hulls and everything…." He seized her hand so he could admire them. It took him a moment to remember he shouldn't do that, either, and dropped her hand on the table. He hid his hands in his lap.

"I felt like something bright, and they reminded me of you."

Her smile could have lit up the whole universe. All except the part where he was.

"How old are you, Franny?"

She blinked. "It's a bit late to be asking that now, isn't it? I mean, checking if I'm jail bait after we've done the deed."

He felt his cheeks grow hot. "Please. I need to know."

She blew out an angry breath. "Fine. I'm twenty-one. The second oldest in the collective, after Donna, of course."

He didn't know what to think. "Just that someone told me there were children in Star Farm, and I was worried…"

She snorted. "You thought I was a kid? How many kids can make croissants and tarts and bread better than you?"

"Well, none," he admitted.

"We were kids when we signed up for

the program. All under eighteen, though Rue and I turned eighteen soon after we were accepted. We sneaked out of the training college and down to the local pub for a drink on my birthday. The beer was disgusting and the wine was worse, but we managed to choke down a glass each before we snuck back. We were in so much trouble when we got back, no one was allowed to leave the college after that."

"Are any of you still under eighteen?" he persisted. He had to know.

"No. Iva's the youngest – she was fifteen when she joined the program. I'm not sure if she lied about her age or if she just got special permission or something. Anyway, she had her birthday a few weeks ago. She's eighteen and legally an adult. She can drink all the foul beer she wants." Franny gestured at a blonde girl with a large glass of beer in her hand.

"And she's looking for her match here, in this pub?"

Franny shrugged. "Some of us are. Some of us might have already found ours. And some…some of the girls are just fulfilling the terms of our contract." She couldn't blame them for it. She wasn't the only one here who wasn't cut out for farm life.

"What contract?"

"The one we signed back on Earth, of course. In return for being transported to the Colony, we are required to perform ten years' labour and bear four children. This is Donna's way of helping them get a head start on the children part of things, I guess."

Oh, stars. Allie had been right. Sexual slavery, indentured labour, child labour…all of it.

"Is that why you…picked me? To get you pregnant?"

She screwed up her nose. "Fuck, no. I was supposed to stay here and meet men, in the hope of meeting someone I might want to spend my life with. Instead, I followed you on a whim, to see your bakery. What we did after…well, I definitely remember you being pretty insistent on contraception, and I wasn't going to object. Maybe I should have. Maybe I should never have gone with you. Maybe this was all a mistake because you're a suspicious arse

—"

Claw's comm beeped. An urgent call from Fang.

"Hey, you remember when you asked me if I'd done anything illegal?" Fang asked.

Claw rose. "I need to take this." He bolted outside.

"Yeah?" he asked.

"What if I think I've signed an illegal contract?"

This was definitely the night for dodgy contracts. Claw sighed. "You'd better let me take a look at it."

A moment later, the document appeared on the screen.

Allie had been so, so right. Sexual slavery…and they were selling the girls. Fang, fool that he was, had bloody bought one.

And Talon fancied one of the girls, too…worse, he was working at Star Farm with his birds.

"Stars. We need to tell Talon about this, before he does something stupid."

"Why? Where is he?"

"At Star Farm."

TWENTY-ONE

He ran home. The moment the door closed behind him, Claw commed Talon. The call connected, but no one spoke. Claw waited for a long moment, before he said, "Stars take it, Talon, I know you're there. This won't wait until you wake up. I need you to get out of Star Farm immediately, do you hear me? Pack up your birds and go. Don't have any more contact with anyone from Star Farm. Especially not the girls."

He might not even be there. He might not be listening. But Claw had to warn him. To convince him not to do anything as stupid as Fang already had. What had Allie said? Something about the treaty. He didn't understand it, but it had scared him enough. Maybe it would work on Talon, too.

"Look, Talon, there's a reason those girls are isolated at Star Farm. Why they're not supposed to leave. Because if they get out and mix with the general population…the peace treaty, and everything we've built here in the Colony will be put at risk."

For a moment, he thought he heard

someone say something, but then there was silence.

Claw tried again: "If just one of those girls gets out...she could start another war faster than the ice asteroid that destroyed the *Titanic*." He rubbed his eyes. That sounded crazy, even to him. He waited another long moment, before ending the call.

Then he called Allie. Last time, he'd been too busy worrying about being a paedophile to get a proper explanation from her. This time, he wouldn't let Allie go until she told him why Franny – sweet, bubbly, sexy Franny – was such a threat to the Colony.

TWENTY-TWO

"Hi, Orson." A baby began to wail.

"Are you busy?" He didn't want to bother her when she had a screaming baby to deal with.

"No, I've just finished feeding Cece. She's screaming because she wants more, greedy little minx. Maybe it's time we started feeding her something more than milk."

Claw didn't know a thing about babies. "Okay."

"What's up? You marked the call as urgent."

"You were right. About all of it. The girls in Star Farm were recruited as kids back on Earth, they signed indentured labour contracts, including bearing children, and they went to the Intergalactic Dating Agency to find baby daddies." Then he remembered the contract Fang had signed. "Or buyers."

"What?" So Allie hadn't known about the worst of it.

"The woman in charge of the school or the farm or whatever it is, sold one of the girls as a sex slave."

"How do you know this? Did you see

it?"

Claw sighed. "Because I've seen the contract he signed. My friend's the one who bought her."

"Your friend you thought was a good guy? Orson Claw, do you have any idea how many sexual predators get called good guys by their male friends, who actually don't know anything about them?"

"It's Fang! He is a good guy!"

Allie was silent for a moment. "Fang? As in Dr Fang? My dentist?"

"Yes?" How was Claw supposed to know if Fang was her dentist?

"You're telling me my vampire dentist bought a sex slave?"

He wasn't sure how to answer that. "Maybe?" That seemed safe.

"Stars, Orson. This is an even bigger mess than I thought."

In the silence, Claw summoned his courage. "You know how you said the Star Farm girls could destroy the peace treaty, and start a new war? What exactly did you mean by that?"

Another long pause. "Are you alone? Somewhere where you can't be overheard?"

"I'm in the bakery, and of course I'm alone. The girl I wanted to spend my evening with is apparently such a huge threat to the Colony that she needs to be locked up!"

"Okay, I'm in the bedroom. With the door closed, so no one can hear me. And did you just say that you've bought one of the Star Farm girls, too? You're a lawyer, Orson! You know that's all kind of illegal! How old is she?"

Claw let out a breath he hadn't known he'd been holding. "Franny's twenty-one. She turned eighteen before she even left Earth. All the girls are adults now, she said. Even the youngest. That's why they were in that pub."

"You still bought her."

"Two strawberry tarts are hardly a fair price for a human being," Claw shot back.

"Two…what? Did you say tarts? You've bought two girls now?"

"No! I…never mind. I haven't bought anyone. I might have…taken one of the girls home with me for the night, but everything we did was consensual."

"Indentured labour, sexual

slavery…there's no way you can know that. If she believes the farm owns her body, then she's already been coerced. There's no way she can give consent under those circumstances."

He thought of Franny, of how she'd begged for him. "She did. You've got to believe me, Allie. Look, ask her if you like. Everything we did was consensual. I'm sure Fang's the same. He's a vampire, for stars' sake. He has to get consent before he can bite anyone, or take a single drop of blood. He wouldn't have touched the girl without her consent."

"You don't know that. You can't know that. Stars, Orson…"

"It's Claw!" he exploded.

"All right, Claw! You've really dipped

your dick in it this time. You and your friend. Wait, didn't you say there were three of you?"

"Talon. The griffon meowl keeper. I called him the moment I knew Star Farm was suspicious, to warn him away from them."

"And what did he say?"

Claw hesitated. "I don't know. The call went through, so I think he heard me, but I can't be sure. I told him to leave the farm and stay away from the girls. Sometimes he keeps his comm on auto-answer when he's in griffon form, though, because it's hard to manipulate the screen when you have claws." He knew all about that, though he couldn't remember the last time he'd shifted fully into bear form. Maybe a few months back, when he'd gone for a run in the Arbor Dome.

"So you're telling me all three of you have been sleeping with sex slaves, when you were supposed to be investigating this mess?"

When she put it like that…

"You asked me to investigate. I did!"

"I also told you to be careful. Stars…you know I'm going to have to call the Watch about this, don't you? They're Humans. It's outside of my jurisdiction. You're on your own on this one."

"Wait…what? The Watch? You're going to have me arrested?"

That was definitely not what he'd planned for tonight.

"No, you dickhead. The Watch will go

in and take a look, talk to the woman in charge of the farm. They'll probably want to talk to you, too, so you can give them your evidence in person. Depending on what you tell them, they might decide to arrest you, but that's on them. I'm only responsible for Mer justice. Humans…aren't my problem."

Claw blew out a breath. He'd heard horror stories about Mer justice. He'd take a life in prison over Mer justice any day of the week.

A sudden thought hit him. "Hey, you still haven't told me why these girls are so dangerous."

Allie sighed. "Promise you won't freak out, okay?"

And she told him.

"Blithering black holes, are you

serious?"

Of course she was.

TWENTY-THREE

Franny finished dinner early, so she never saw the newcomers. She was almost done stripping the strawberry nail polish from her fingernails when the other girls trooped into the common room, debating who the strangers might be.

"It was two women in uniform,"

Kalina said. Her eyes lit up when she saw Franny had her nail kit out. "Ooh, are you painting nails tonight?"

With the mood she was in, Franny was likely to paint everyone's nails matte black. She couldn't believe she'd fallen for such an arsehole. She'd been on the point of telling him she loved him and wanted more, and he'd just walked out of the pub. No goodbye, no second glance, nothing. Like he didn't care about her at all, and she'd just been a night's fun to him. Fun and free labour, no less.

And all those questions, like he was more interested in Star Farm than her.

It was clear she meant nothing to him, so he should be less than nothing to her. She'd forget all about him, and that would be that.

"I'm taking paint off tonight. Maybe by the weekend, I'll be up for making things pretty again," Franny said.

Kalina sighed, and slumped onto the couch. "Wish I'd thought to bring nail polish in my personal items. I packed clothes, and I haven't had anywhere to wear them, what with us wearing uniforms all day."

"Didn't you wear that pretty black dress to the pub?" Franny asked. Ha, matte black nails would have matched the dress. But it would have been improved by a light coast of clear gloss with diamond or silver glitter. Something to catch the light, to give the tiniest hint of colour as if to say life wasn't all darkness.

Kalina shook her head. "No, that was

what Donna gave me to wear. I didn't know we were allowed to wear our own stuff, but the dress Donna loaned me was a designer label. Better than anything I brought."

Come to think of it, so had the one she'd given Franny to wear. She hadn't given it a second thought at the time, because she'd had a couple of nice dresses for school formals and graduation and stuff, but where had Donna gotten them from? Surely she hadn't lugged a wardrobe full of fancy clothes halfway across the galaxy just for them? They had to have weighed way more than Donna's personal allowance.

"So did the strangers come to see Donna?" Franny asked, suddenly curious.

"Yep. They asked to see her, but she's not back yet."

Ah, that's right. Franny hadn't seen Donna at any of the meals today, which was unusual. Maybe she'd had important things to do in the Colony. Or maybe she'd just taken a day off – her first in the year they'd been in the Colony.

"So did they just leave?" Franny asked. "Say they'd come back later?"

Kalina grinned. "Nope. They insisted on seeing whoever was in charge, because this wouldn't wait, so they ducked into Donna's office with Flora and closed the door."

"So we just have to wait until they leave and then ask Flora what they wanted?" Franny said.

"Like Flora will tell us. Isn't she

Donna's niece or something? She'd never sell out her family's secrets."

Actually, Flora had barely known Donna when her parents died and she'd become her ward, Flora had confessed to Franny once when she'd painted her nails. Then she'd been accepted into the Farm Stars program and not seen Donna again until they woke up here. Sure, Flora was the one placed in charge when Donna left the farm, and she'd been the one at the pub, making sure everyone was there when it was time to go home, but it wasn't like Flora wanted the responsibility.

"I heard some man shouting to Donna about the blonde girl last night. He was at the pub, too. Do you think he came here looking for Dani?" Kalina asked.

Franny shrugged. "Dani or Iva. Who knows? Actually, I haven't seen either of them tonight. Have you?"

"Iva's probably in solitary again. You know she likes to piss Donna off."

Franny's gaze drifted around the room. "Rue's not here, either. I don't think I've seen her all day, and that's really weird, because she's all about the farming, usually."

"She might still be in the dining room. Donna keeps putting her on cleanup duty."

Yeah, because if Donna put Rue in solitary, no one would have any idea what to do around the farm. Donna or Flora might be nominally in charge, but Rue really ran this place. Or at least the farm part of it. Franny hoped she got her own piece of land one day. It wasn't fair what had happened to her parents, or their farm.

But Rue hadn't been at dinner.

Donna was gone. Iva, Rue and Dani were missing. And now there were strangers on the farm?

Something was going on, and Franny intended to find out what.

As if by magic, Flora appeared.

Franny waved. "You look like your nails need some colour."

Actually, she looked like she needed a stiff drink and a holiday, but a manicure was the best Franny could offer.

"Yes, please," Flora said, dragging a seat over beside Franny's. She knew the drill. "I think I've chewed off nearly all the polish, wishing Donna was here to meet the Watch instead of me."

Franny pulled out a file and began buffing Flora's nails. No point painting them if they weren't the right shape. "So is that who our visitors were? What's the Watch?"

Flora sighed as she relaxed back in her chair. "They're sort of the Colony police, or that's what they said. Our visitors were Detectives Violet and Minali, and they wanted to see all the farm's paperwork. All our contracts and financial records and personal records and procedures and…in the end, I just gave them everything. I mean, I do the book keeping, but Donna deals with all the other stuff. Then they asked me how old the girls were, like it wasn't already listed in our files. So I told them from

Iva at eighteen to you, me and Rue at twenty-one."

"When was your birthday?"

"Yesterday. Donna must have forgotten, because she didn't arrange cake…"

At Star Farm, cake was a chocolate flavoured protein bar with a candle stuck in it.

One day, Franny would bake proper cakes for everyone on their birthdays. Even Donna.

"Happy birthday, then. Why didn't you say something yesterday?"

Flora shrugged. "I guess it felt weird, preparing my own cake instead of having someone bring it out to me. I usually do it for everyone else, but I felt silly doing it for myself."

"Right, what colour do you want? I'm thinking…a lovely sky blue base coat, with a different birthday balloon on each finger. What do you think? I mean, I could do candles instead…"

Flora beamed. "Balloons would be perfect."

"So did the Watch say why they wanted all the farm's paperwork?" Franny asked as she stroked the blue gloss down Flora's nails.

Flora shrugged again. "They wouldn't say much. Something about legal irregularities, or possible ones. They made it sound like someone had forgotten to dot an i or cross a t or something. They said not to worry."

Like the lawyers had told Mum not to worry about her father's divorce, because it couldn't possibly affect them, and then they'd lost the bakery.

"Have you seen Dani or Rue or Iva today?" Franny set Flora's hand down on the table, glistening with blue polish, and reached for the other one.

"No, none of them. Oh, Iva's in solitary again. Donna put her in there for not making a match at the dating thing the other night. Funny, seeing as Iva was so eager to go, but she rejected every man who came near her. Kept saying she had particular tastes, whatever that means." Flora rolled her eyes. "I should probably let her out. I know I'd be going crazy in the dark, all alone, but Donna insists it's for our own good. Teaches obedience, or some shit like that. I'm pretty sure sensory deprivation is a kind of torture, and illegal everywhere except here."

"Maybe that's what the Watch is worried about. They might take away the stasis pods, so Donna can't confine us to solitary again." Hey, she could hope. "Iva can probably wait another fifteen minutes, or until your nails dry, though. I think she actually likes the pods."

"You know, you might be right. You know what she said once? It gave her the time and privacy to masturbate. I expected Donna to be shocked, but she just shook her head. The next day, she announced the Intergalactic Dating Agency thing."

Where Franny had met Claw and his incredible cock, before he'd stomped on her heart.

"Did you find your perfect match at one of the speed dating events?" Franny asked as she began on the balloons. A rainbow of colours would look best, she decided. With black strings.

Flora's cheeks turned faintly pink. "I didn't get a chance to meet anyone. I was so busy supervising, I didn't get to meet any of the men. Donna wanted notes on each of the men, so I spent most of my time talking to Vertumnus, the faun administrator at the pub. He had files on everyone, and he was only too happy to share."

"Sounds like Mr Tumnus took quite a liking to you. Did you return his regard, by any chance?" Franny asked.

Flora was definitely blushing. "No, of course not! And it's Vertumnus, though he did say I could call him Tumnus if I wanted."

She had it bad. Lucky Flora. "I hope if you do call him that, he's been good enough to you to deserve it. I mean, some men think that if they can just get between your legs, they actually deserve to be there, when the truth is that all they deserve is their own hand."

Flora looked like she wanted to slap her, but she didn't dare until her nails were dry. "Franny! You can't say things like that. One of the younger girls might hear."

Franny snorted. "What, Iva? She'd probably tell you the going rate for screaming a man's name is three orgasms in a row from oral sex or five from digital penetration. Or something equally technical."

"Digital penetration? Is that…?" Flora looked terribly confused.

Franny was pretty sure she was still a virgin.

She wiggled her fingers. "Fucking you with his fingers. It helps if he has thick fingers. Or long ones. Or even both. But even if he has small hands, as long as he can find your clit, he could still be good."

"Franny!" Flora hissed.

"You should probably let Iva out soon. I must be missing her, if I'm the one delivering all the dirty comments."

Flora examined her nails. "They look lovely. Thank you."

"Happy belated birthday. Give them another five minutes, and you should be good to go," Franny said, putting the bottles away.

"Do you really think Donna's doing something illegal here?" Flora asked. "It's just that…she's all I've got, and if I lose her, I'll be alone again."

"Whether she is or she isn't, it's not your problem, it's hers," Franny said. "And what do you mean you'll be alone? You're a Farm Star, just like the rest of us. You've got more sisters than anyone in the universe could ever ask for. We all signed up for the same thing. A new life, a new family, here in the Altan System. We're all each other has, and we'll kick the arse of anyone, alien or otherwise, who tries to tear us apart."

Flora perked up. "You would?"

"Definitely. Rue would probably run them over with some farm equipment,

Iva would threaten them with kinky sex that she knows far too much about, Kalina would give them a stern talking to and Linnaea would probably burst into tears until they begged her to stop, but…well, we'd all raise hell, in our own ways."

"Then I hope there's nothing illegal about us owning Star Farm. I'd hate for us to lose our home." Flora thanked her for the manicure, and headed off to rescue Iva.

Of course, that only left Franny with her thoughts. She wouldn't mind losing Star Farm. She'd march up to the Colony Administration, wherever that was, and ask for a bakery. She'd do a damn better job than Claw, and they'd given him one.

More likely it was some technicality in

their contracts. Now that could be good. If her contract was voided, then she wouldn't have to work for ten years, or have children for the Colony. She'd be free to walk away from the farm and…demand a bakery.

Just as long as she and the other girls hadn't done something illegal. After all, who knew what laws the aliens had brought to the Colony?

TWENTY-FOUR

For two days, Claw had sweated and worried and sweated all over again, waiting for a visit from the Watch. But when two women in black walked into the bakery to buy the last two remaining cakes for the day, he was actually surprised.

"Mr Orson Claw, right?" one asked,

biting into her croissant.

He nodded. "Claw, like the name on the sign out the front. That's right."

"Or the pastry," said the second one, holding up her bear claw before she took a bite. "Ooh, this is good. Are you sure you don't want half?"

The first woman had already wolfed down the croissant. "I'm good," she mumbled around a mouthful of food.

"Mr Claw, we're here to ask you a few questions about the Intergalactic Dating Agency and Star Farm."

Then the croissant woman introduced herself as Detective Minali, while her claw-chomping colleague was Detective Violet.

Claw sighed. "I'd better close up for the day, then."

Then he took them upstairs to his apartment and told them everything.

To their credit, they mostly just listened. Occasionally, one of them asked a question to clarify what he'd said, but he was the one doing the talking, while they took notes on their tablets. Finally, Minali set hers down.

"So, what you've told us is that you already know a great deal about both Star Farm and the Intergalactic Dating Agency, and you have a vested interest in seeing that those girls are treated fairly and justly, and reparations are made for any wrongs done to them."

Stiffly, Claw nodded. If he weren't a law abiding man, he'd happily strangle whoever had made seventeen-year-old Franny sign that contract. Or feed them piece by piece to Talon's flock of birds.

The two detectives shared a glance.

"Good," Violet said. "Because my friend Allie recommended you as the perfect contract lawyer to look these over and comment on their legality in the Altan System." She tapped away at her tablet, then stabbed at it one final time with her finger. "There. Sent."

Claw glanced at his own tablet and his eyes widened. She'd sent him a folder containing dozens, if not hundreds of files. "This will take months!" he protested.

"You have a week. After that, we're going to have to release the Star Farm girls into the wider community. As it is, they're being held prisoner without even the suspicion of a crime. It's up to you to find out who's innocent and who's guilty, and what crime they've committed."

"I'm not that kind of lawyer!" Claw protested.

Violet gave him a sympathetic smile. "We don't have the luxury of a Central Intelligence here, so we kind of have to wing it. Even if you could just tell me who the victims are, it would help."

He stared at the long list of documents. "I might be able to do that."

Both women rose. "If there's anything else you need, just contact us, Mr Claw. Or contact Flora at Star Farm. She's been very helpful. As you are helping the Watch in an official capacity, you can requisition any information you need from anyone in the Colony to help us on this case."

He ushered them out, his mind whirling while he hoped he mumbled something polite in farewell.

When they were gone, he sat down on the couch, staring at the tablet in his hands. He'd planned to go straight to bed, but…

This was for Franny. Setting her free.

So he set to work.

TWENTY-FIVE

It took Claw three days to go through everything. It turned out a lot of the documents were copies of the same contracts, which all the girls had signed. How any lawyer could have written such a document in the first place…Claw could only shake his head.

What he couldn't find was anything

related to the Intergalactic Dating Agency. Even when he called Star Farm, Flora told him she had nothing else she hadn't already sent him. "All the contracts for that were held by Falcon Han at the One Shot Cantina, and his administrator, Vertumnus," she told him.

So Claw changed into clean clothes (he couldn't remember how long he'd been wearing these ones) and headed to the pub.

He remembered the bar staff from the first night — a stringy-looking old man with a face like a hawk, and a fussy faun who'd had a tablet glued to his hand the whole night.

But when he stepped inside the empty pub, he found neither of them.

Behind the bar stood a man who'd

look more in character as a bouncer than a barman. Claw himself was a big man, but in a fair fight, he wasn't sure whether he or this man would win.

Luckily, he wasn't here for a fight.

"Hi, I'm looking for Falcon Han," Claw said.

The barman set down the glass he'd been polishing. "I hate to tell you, but he's dead."

Claw froze. "He's what?"

"Dead. Died of a heart attack. It's kind of sad, really. It looks like he went out back to put out the rubbish, and collapsed behind the bins. Nobody found his body until the scheduled pickup a week later, and then he was too far gone for anyone to help him. I'm the new owner. Name's Hercules." He extended a meaty hand.

Claw shook. Firm, but not intimidating. Like Hercules didn't have anything to prove. Claw could respect that.

"Nice to meet you and all, but I'm here to review some documentation about the Intergalactic Dating Agency, something Falcon Han was involved with, hosted here at the Cantina. Any chance you'd be willing to show me the contracts?"

Hercules shrugged. "I don't know anything about that, but you're welcome to take a look in the office. You won't need a password – I've left everything unlocked."

He seemed helpful enough, so Claw set to work before Hercules changed his mind.

Actually, everything was pretty clear. Just like the men who'd signed up for the Agency's services, Star Farm Collective had signed for its girls. As adult members of the Collective, that was all legal and above board.

Claw breathed a sigh of relief. On paper, at least, Franny had been here of her own volition, and free to do as she chose.

But when he considered the contracts she'd signed with Star Farm…now that was another can of worms entirely.

TWENTY-SIX

"So it looks like the only guilty party I can find is this Donna woman, at least here in the Colony, and whoever put together the Farm Stars program in the first place, back on Earth. It looks like some sort of foundation, and I found a list of names, but none of them appear to live in the Colony," Claw finished, looking from Minali to Violet and back again. He wouldn't want to play poker against either of these women.

"That list of names matches some of the original *Genesis* colonists. They were all killed in the terrorist attack on the space elevator. They never made it to Exodus," Minali said. "They were all rich, powerful men who'd put a lot of money into building *Genesis*. The kind who could hire the best lawyers to ensure they got off scot free, no matter what crimes they were accused of. The Colony is a better place without them, I'm sure."

Claw whistled. "I'll say. What about Donna?"

Violet frowned. "She's disappeared. No one's seen her since before we first visited the farm. It's like someone warned her we were coming."

Claw threw his hands up. "Don't look at me. I want answers from this woman as much as you. The things she's done…"

"Yes, and when we find her, justice will be done," Violet said darkly. "But in the meantime, can I confirm that all the girls presently living at Star Farm are innocent of any crime, to the best of your knowledge, and are all victims in this matter?"

He didn't know all the girls, but… "Based on the documents you've given me, yes. They were coerced into signing contracts of questionable legality, and then forced to hold to the terms of that contract. The only good news I can see is that the bonuses they were due as First Settlers, as well as the salaries they earned while working at the farm, have been held in trust in the Star Farm Collective accounts. So even without this Donna, there are funds available to compensate them for the theft and what amounted to slave labour."

"Good. So, you're available to brief the Star Farm residents tomorrow on their legal status, and options?"

"Me?"

"Of course it has to be you. You're the most qualified contract lawyer in the Colony, and the Watch engaged your services to help us in this matter. Do you think I'm going to stand there and answer questions on Colony law and contracts? No, we need a lawyer for that, and that's you."

"But…"

"Five in the evening at Star Farm, Mr Claw. Don't be late."

Claw sighed. He'd be there.

Maybe he'd even get to see Franny again. Not that she'd want to see him.

TWENTY-SEVEN

They'd assembled in the dining room to hear what the grave-looking man had to say. Flora just kept shaking her head, muttering to herself, convinced they were about to hear something terrible.

Rue and Dani had reappeared, but they both sat off to the side, separate from everyone else, and beaming like they'd both won the lottery.

As for the other girls…the room was filled with chattering and whispering, as everyone wondered what they'd hear.

Finally, the grave-looking man hushed everyone. "My name is Ira, and I'm the Commander of the Watch here in the Colony. I am…for lack of a better phrase, the law in these parts. So it falls to me to tell you what I must today. I'm sorry for those of you who might already know what I have to tell you, but I need to make sure everyone is on the same page. So if you'll forgive me…I have a short history lecture for you."

Grumbling for a few seconds, before everyone fell silent.

"You were all recruited for the Farm Stars program. The program wanted fit, healthy girls aged between sixteen and eighteen, with few family connections, preferably a trade or an interest in farming, and a willingness to go into space. On acceptance, you were required to sign contracts that bound you to ten years of labour in the Colony and the live birth of four children. You were subjected to rigorous training on Earth, before being sent up to Exodus, where you were placed in stasis in the not yet completed colony ship, *Genesis*. Right?"

Heads nodded. Even Franny couldn't fault him.

"After you were placed in stasis, there was a terrorist attack on the space elevator, and Exodus. The space station was damaged, and the space elevator was destroyed. Those aboard the Exodus had no choice but to board the *Genesis* and come to the Altan System, though they were not the colonists who'd paid for passage, like your benefactors, who were killed in the attack, or indentured labourers, like yourselves. They were construction crews and station staff."

More whispering and alarmed looks. Claw had told her some of this before, but she hadn't believed him.

"These are some images of the damage done by the attack."

Gasps rose from the girls as Franny couldn't deny it any more. Half of Exodus was gone, and the space elevator…God, you could see the impact crater it had made on Earth.

"When the *Genesis* arrived here in the Altan System, they found they weren't alone. The *Titanic* had also arrived, and both Humans and Titans began to colonise the system. The Titans came from the Titan System, living on the planet Tito and its moon, Alba. Both were run by a sentient artificial intelligence known as the Central Intelligence. Until it turned hostile, and the robots it controlled began to kill Titans instead of helping them. Those who could, fled to the *Titanic*. The *Titanic* came here."

Franny still wanted to laugh at such a terrible name for a ship.

"When Humans and Titans met, war was almost inevitable. Both races wanted this system for themselves. After years of fighting, we declared a truce, and after much negotiation, hammered out a treaty. We now share the Altan System, with each race taking three planets, with the only shared planet, New Hope, the seventh, outermost one, the site of the city we call the Colony. A city that the citizens of Altan believe was built by a combination of Titan and Human labour, after the treaty was signed."

The crowd erupted in cries of denial. Even Franny was out of her seat, and she couldn't say why. The war and the terrorist attack she could believe, but this…you only had to look at the Colony to know Humans couldn't have built this.

Ira signalled for silence. After a long moment, he got it. "You ladies are some of the few people in the Altan System who know the truth. The Colony was not built by Human or Titan hands, but by an artificial intelligence with 3D printers that was sent ahead of the *Genesis*, to build the city before any colonists arrived. A city run by an AI, with robots to serve the colonists. Just like the one on Tito, before everything went wrong."

He waited for a moment, then continued, "The city was constructed, then hidden with experimental stealth technology, so it was invisible until a fighter plane collided with the shield and two ships, one Human and one Titan, witnessed the appearance of the city on an otherwise barren planet. It began broadcasting advertising communications to the ships, telling them about the better world that had been built for them in the Colony.

"A small group of explorers were sent into the city to investigate. They thought aliens had constructed it, but the AI informed them otherwise. A construction team was put together, consisting mostly of Humans, with a Titan consultant, to work with the AI and its army of robots, to turn the city into what we know today as the Colony. After which, all the robots were destroyed, and the AI was removed from control of the city."

Yes, they all knew this. Or most of it, anyway. Donna had told them their city had been modified to accommodate their new alien neighbours.

"But the peace treaty between our peoples, Titan and Human, is contingent on no AI or robot presence anywhere in the Altan System. If the Titan population were to find out that this city was constructed by them, even if they are not present now, there would be war."

Franny could see why. Claw had lost his parents to killer robots. He wouldn't want to live in a city built by them.

"By some strange twist of fate, you have this knowledge of what amounts to one of the greatest state secrets in the Altan System. Before you can leave Star Farm and mingle with the rest of the Colony population, I must ask you to sign a nondisclosure agreement."

"And what if we don't?" Kalina shouted.

Ira grimaced. "If you refuse to sign the agreement, then I will be forced to place you back in stasis indefinitely. Your pod will be moved to a secure facility…"

"So all we have to do is not talk about robots or AI or how this city was built, yeah?" Kalina asked.

Ira nodded.

"Anyone got a problem with that? Anyone actually want to talk about robots or any of that shit?" Heads shook. Not everyone, but most of them. Kalina nodded. "Right, where do we sign, then?"

They all lined up, and within minutes, every contract was signed. Even Franny didn't hesitate.

If they wanted to leave Star Farm and mingle with the rest of the Colony…oh, hell yes!

"If you violate this contract, you

commit treason, and the punishment is severe," Ira said, but no one seemed to be listening any more.

"What about leaving Star Farm? We still have the other contracts we signed!" Kalina shouted.

Ira coughed. "This is where I introduce you to our legal expert, Mr Orson Claw."

Wait…what?

TWENTY-EIGHT

Claw knew there were other people in the crowd, but the moment he saw Franny's face, the room might as well have been empty. She was the reason he was here, why he'd worked so hard. She definitely didn't look happy to see him, but right now he couldn't allow himself to think about that.

"When you signed the contracts for the Farm Stars program back on Earth, you weren't legally adults. Which means…under Earth laws and the ones here in the Altan System…the contracts you signed back then are not legally binding. Even if your parents had signed them for you, as your legal guardians, the moment you turned eighteen, the contracts were voided. Because the records now show all of you are most definitely adults over the legal age of eighteen, any contract you sign now, including the non disclosure agreement, is legally binding. The Farm Stars program that you signed up for does not exist in the Altan System."

Shocked exclamations came from the audience, but Franny just looked like someone had lifted a weight off her shoulders. Like she'd already half expected this.

"However, while the program might not exist, Star Farm is a very real place, and the Star Farm Collective, which owns it, is a legal entity. When it was created, you were all listed as members of the Collective, allowing the Collective to collect your salary and bonuses on your behalf. From what I can tell, those credits are still sitting in the Collective's accounts, untouched. As adult citizens in the Colony, you are entitled to remove your share of the overall funds should you choose to leave the Collective."

He took a deep breath. "This is where you have a choice. You are free citizens of the Colony. As such, you are entitled to accommodation, education, employment and ration bars in accordance with your family status. You also have leave entitlements, should you wish to use them. In the coming days, Colony Administration will send some representatives with whom you may discuss your options, should you wish to leave the Collective.

"Which leads me to the most difficult decision you will have to make. Though you did not sign any agreements about this, you are listed as members of the Star Farm Collective. If you should all decide to dissolve the Collective and go your own separate ways, you will no longer be able to stay here at Star Farm, as it will be reallocated to other farmers who wish to use the facility. If some of you wish to continue with the Collective, and retain Star Farm, then you will need to write a new agreement and sign this. In fact, should some of you choose to continue as part of the Collective, you will need to completely rewrite all agreements, contracts and procedures, in line with Colony legal requirements.

"Any contract which was not entered into in accordance with the laws of the Altan System is null and void, and any credits which changed hands in line with those contracts will be returned to the original owner, unless the payment is for services rendered, in which case the matter must be negotiated with the person who rendered the services."

He coughed, unable to stop his eyes from shifting to the girl Fang had bought. She looked cheerful enough. Maybe she knew just how much Fang had paid for her, and was considering what she might buy with it. Fang was lucky he hadn't been arrested for doing something so stupid.

"You will have four weeks in which to decide. Any questions?"

TWENTY-NINE

Franny wasn't sure whether she wanted to hit Claw…or hug him. She'd hardly dared hope that the contract might be cancelled, yet here he was, telling her it didn't exist.

Even better, now Donna couldn't stop her from leaving and starting up her own bakery in the Colony.

She would, too. She'd tell the Colony Administration that she was a way better baker than Claw, and how competition was good for business and the community.

And maybe, when her bakery was established as the best pastryhouse in the Colony, she might find another man to bend her over the worktable when all the work was done, thrust his massive cock inside her and keep going until she screamed in ecstasy. Not once, but over and over and…

Who was she kidding? Claw was the only man she wanted, and his was the only cock that haunted both her waking hours and her dreams.

THIRTY

"Do we still have to bear babies for the Colony?" one girl asked.

"Not if you don't want to. You aren't bound by that old contract any more. It is up to you, as responsible adults, who, if anyone, you choose to share your bodies with, and whether you have children. There is no pressure to have a family. If you might have already found someone you'd like to date or maybe even something more, you're free to choose whether you want to be with that person."

He couldn't help but look at Franny then, wishing he could tell her that he longed with all his heart for her to choose him, just like she did that first night in the pub.

"What if we want training to take on a new job — like if we want to study to be a nurse or a midwife. Would the Colony allow that?"

Interesting. That was the girl Fang had bought. She didn't need a job, not with his money, but not everyone wanted to sit around, doing nothing.

"That's absolutely something the

Colony Administration would be interested in helping you with – including housing near the hospital, if you want to stay in Metropolis City instead of one of the satellite domes. There are brochures on the table over there, describing each of the domes and the climate and recreation options they each offer. Of course, you are free to enter any dome and any public area you wish at any time, but you might be partial to sporting events, or walking in the woods, or lakeside living, in which case you'd choose the dome that matches what you like best."

"What if we're already trained in a trade, and want to set up our own business?"

He'd know her voice anywhere. His

eyes met hers and he couldn't look away.

THIRTY-ONE

When he was too busy looking at her with naked longing to answer, Franny forced herself to ask the question again. "What if we're already trained in a trade and want to start our own business?"

His face fell, like she'd driven a dagger right into his heart. "Then the Colony Administration will help you find premises, and assign you the resources you need to start that business. You'll need to keep applying for each week's resource allocation, depending on what's available, but that's the same for any business, anywhere. The only difference here is that if you're missing half your milk order, it's usually because there isn't any more milk in the Colony this week, and there won't be any more until next week."

Next week. God, what she'd give to see him again next week. To work beside him in the same kitchen, stopping for a quickie, then back to work again. All night. Every night.

She shouldn't even be thinking it. He'd been investigating Star Farm all this time, and she'd only been a means to an end, but that end had been to tear up her contract, to free her from her indenture. She wanted to be mad at him, but she also wanted to jump on him, climb him like a tree and…

Franny closed her eyes. She was not going to have sex in public with this man. No matter how much she wanted to.

"What if…what if we wanted to enter into a partnership with an existing business, to widen the range of products that business might be able to offer, and improve them?" she asked.

His mouth opened, but no words came out. Almost like he wanted it as much as she did.

"As a free citizen of the Colony, any partnership you wished to enter into would be entirely your choice. I imagine any business owner you wished to partner with would be extremely lucky to have you."

His eyes begged, and she knew she was lost. Damn puppy dog eyes.

She laughed. "As long as he remembers how lucky he is, every day, I think I could work with that."

"Well, if there are no more questions…" Claw glanced around, but there were no more raised hands. "Then thank you for not falling asleep during my briefing, and good luck with the decisions you'll be making in the near future."

Franny rose from her seat, dashing to meet Claw before he could leave.

"Did you really mean what you said? You want to work with me?" he asked.

"Well, someone's got to teach you how to bake properly," she teased. "But yes, I think we work well together. I like working with you and…as long as there's plenty of good, hot sex and you bake me croissants for breakfast every morning, maybe we could even make the partnership more than just a business one."

His eyes shone. "I didn't think you'd forgive me for how rude I was to you the last time I saw you at the pub. I wanted nothing more than to take you back home with me, like the other nights we spent together, but I knew I couldn't until you were free of that indenture contract. Then when I found a way to dissolve the contract, I baked you something, but I wasn't game to bring it here in case you threw it in my face. Because I couldn't know whether you were free to choose until you were no longer bound by that stars-crossed contract."

"I might have," she admitted. "There I was all ready to tell you I wanted more than just the occasional meetup in the pub, and you just left. I was pretty pissed off. Even tonight, there were a few minutes there where I'd decided to set up a new bakery, as your competition, and steal all your customers." She inclined her head. "What did you bake, anyway?"

"I discovered there's something called a frangipane tart. I made the tart casing according to your recipe, of course, which is far superior to any other…"

"Of course."

"I filled it with frangipane, which is a smooth, sweet almond paste, which would remind me of you even if it weren't named after you…and then the fruit delivery arrived from Eden, and you know what was on top? A single red apple. The Colony's first apple harvest, apparently, and the perfect thing to finish off your tart. Sliced thin, I arranged the apple on top of the tart like the petals of a frangipani flower. If you come home with me tonight after this, I'll show you. No, I'll feed it to you, before you tell me how I could have made it better. And then…well, that will be up to you. I could make a start on your first instalment of breakfast croissants, but I'm never, ever going to say no to hot sex with you. Maybe we could even go upstairs to my bed so we can take our time, if you're going to be staying for breakfast."

Franny threw her arms around his

neck. "I think I'll want to stay forever." Then she kissed him, and he kissed her back, and nothing else in the universe mattered.

THIRTY-TWO

Flora collected up the non disclosure agreements, while everyone else stood around, talking.

"I'm going to train as a midwife. I had my first appointment last week with an amazing midwife named Maya, and she said she's looking for trainees. I won't need my own apartment, because I'll be living with Fang," Dani said.

"I'm going to move in with Claw and help him run his bakery," Franny said.

"Is he as good in bed as he looks?" Rue asked.

Franny beamed. "Better. What about you? What will you do, Rue?"

"I'm partnering with Talon to run his farm. We've already ordered our first flock of emus and some vine stock. I'm not sure how well the emus will get on with his meowls, but it's not like they're going to eat each other, so I'm sure they'll get used to each other eventually."

All eyes turned to Flora. "What are you going to do?"

Flora managed a wan smile. "Well, someone has to stay here and sort things out. Some of the other girls want to stay, too, so I guess I'll be busy rebuilding the Star Farm Collective from the ground up, though with fewer people. You'd be welcome if you want, Rue, even if you won't live here."

Rue nodded thoughtfully. "Maybe. I mean, Star Farm is growing experimental crops for farming Elysium, and I always planned to settle on a planet with breathable air, not a dome like this one. I don't know. I guess I have four weeks to decide, don't I?"

Flora nodded. None of this seemed real. Least of all how she'd become the person in charge. Damn Donna for disappearing. She should be the one dealing with all this, not her.

Ira came to collect the signed agreements. "Is this everyone?"

"No," Flora said sadly. "Iva's still missing."

Ira looked alarmed. "There's a Farm Stars girl loose in the Colony who hasn't signed the non disclosure agreement? How is that possible?"

Flora just shook her head. "She's missing. None of us know where she is."

Ira pressed his lips together. "Then the Watch will devote every resource we have to finding her. Do you know where she might be?"

"She should be here," Flora said.

"Very well. I'll put my best detectives on it."

Flora only hoped it would be enough.

THIRTY-THREE

In another part of the Colony, Iva woke with a pounding headache. But when she tried to lift her arm to rub her temples, she found her hand cuffed to the bedhead. Both hands, in fact.

"Shit. This can't be good," Iva said.

ABOUT THE AUTHOR

Demelza Carlton has always loved the ocean, but on her first snorkelling trip she found she was afraid of fish.

She has since swum with sea lions, sharks and sea cucumbers and stood on spray drenched cliffs over a seething sea as a seven-metre cyclonic swell surged in, shattering a shipwreck below.

Demelza now lives in Perth, Western Australia, the shark attack capital of the world.

The *Ocean's Gift* series was her first foray into fiction, followed by her suspense thriller *Nightmares* trilogy. She swears the *Mel Goes to Hell* series ambushed her on a crowded train and wouldn't leave her alone.

Want to know more? You can follow Demelza on Facebook, Twitter, YouTube or her website, Demelza Carlton's Place at:

www.demelzacarlton.com

More Books by Demelza Carlton

<u>Colony: Holiday series</u>

Cowboys and Aliens (#1)

Ghost (#2)

Vulcan (#3)

Cupid (#4)

Valentine(#5)

Prometheus (#6)

<u>**Colony: Aqua series**</u>

Halcyon (#1)

Poseidon (#2)

Apollo (#3)

<u>**Colony: Nyx series**</u>

Fang (#1)

Talon (#2)

Claw (#3)

<u>**Siren of Secrets series**</u>

Ocean's Secret (#1)

Ocean's Gift (#2)

Ocean's Infiltrator (#3)

<u>**Nightmares Trilogy**</u>

Nightmares of Caitlin Lockyer (#1)

Necessary Evil of Nathan Miller (#2)

Afterlife of Alana Miller (#3)

<u>**Mel Goes to Hell series**</u>

The Devil's Work (#1)

See You in Hell (#2)

Mel Goes to Hell (#3)

To Hell and Back (#4)

The Holiday From Hell (#5)

All Hell Breaks Loose (#6)

The Devil Goes to Heaven (#7)

<u>**Romance Island Resort series**</u>
Maid for the Rock Star (#1)
The Rock Star's Email Order Bride (#2)
The Rock Star's Virginity (#3)
The Rock Star and the Billionaire (#4)
The Rock Star Wants A Wife (#5)
The Rock Star's Wedding (#6)
Maid for the South Pole (#7)

Romance a Medieval Fairytale series

Enchant: Beauty and the Beast Retold

Dance: Cinderella Retold

Fly: Goose Girl Retold

Revel: Twelve Dancing Princesses Retold

Silence: Little Mermaid Retold

Awaken: Sleeping Beauty Retold

Embellish: Brave Little Tailor Retold

Appease: Princess and the Pea Retold

Blow: Three Little Pigs Retold

Return: Hansel and Gretel Retold

Wish: Aladdin Retold

Melt: Snow Queen Retold

Spin: Rumpelstiltskin Retold

Kiss: Frog Prince Retold

Reflect: Snow White Retold

Roar: Goldilocks Retold

Cobble: Elves and the Shoemaker Retold

Float: Enchanted Horse Retold

Steal: Forty Thieves Retold

Call: Pied Piper Retold

Fall: Scheherazade Retold

Feather: Swan Maidens Retold

Cross: Billy Goats Gruff Retold

Weave: Rapunzel Retold

Claim: Puss in Boots Retold

Curse: Rose Red Retold

Cross: Three Billy Goats Gruff Retold

Weave: Rapunzel Retold

Claim: Puss in Boots Retold

<u>**Heart of Stone series**</u>

Heart of Steel (#0)

Broken Chains (#1)

Broken Bonds (#2)

Broken Dreams (#3)

<u>**Heart of Steel series**</u>

Heart of Steel (#0)

Stone Guardian (#1)

Stone Champion (#2)

Stone Sentinel (#3)

Stone Shadow (#4)